Extinction

by Gabe McKinley

A SAMUEL FRENCH ACTING EDITION

SAMUEL
FRENCH
FOUNDED 1830
NEW YORK HOLLYWOOD LONDON TORONTO

SAMUELFRENCH.COM

ISBN 978-0-573-69850-7   Printed in U.S.A.   #29644

MUSIC USE NOTE

Licensees are solely responsible for obtaining formal written permission from copyright owners to use copyrighted music in the performance of this play and are strongly cautioned to do so. If no such permission is obtained by the licensee, then the licensee must use only original music that the licensee owns and controls. Licensees are solely responsible and liable for all music clearances and shall indemnify the copyright owners of the play and their licensing agent, Samuel French, Inc., against any costs, expenses, losses and liabilities arising from the use of music by licensees.

**IMPORTANT BILLING AND CREDIT
REQUIREMENTS**

All producers of *EXTINCTION must* give credit to the Author of the Play in all programs distributed in connection with performances of the Play, and in all instances in which the title of the Play appears for the purposes of advertising, publicizing or otherwise exploiting the Play and/or a production. The name of the Author *must* appear on a separate line on which no other name appears, immediately following the title and *must* appear in size of type not less than fifty percent of the size of the title type.

EXTINCTION was first produced by Red Dog Squadron at the Elephant Space in Hollywood, California on November 21, 2009. The performance was directed by Wayne Kasserman, with sets by Kurt Boetcher, costumes by Gali Noy, and lighting by Mike Durst. The production stage manager was Susan K. Coulter. The cast was as follows:

MAX . . . . Michael Weston

FINN . . . . James Roday

MISSY . . . . Amanda Detmer

VICTORIA . . . . Stefanie E. Frame

CHARACTERS

FINN, 30's

MAX, 30's

MISSY, 30's

VICTORIA, 20's

SETTING

Adjoining rooms at the Borgata Hotel and Casino in Atlantic City, New Jersey.

TIME

Late Spring/Early Summer

Scene One
"PHYLETIC or The Easy Way"

(Music note: all songs are suggested, not demanded. Music at the beginning of the play could be the Pixies' "Bone Machine," or you might simply have a silent opening to the play.*)

(Adjoining hotel rooms at the Borgata hotel and casino in Atlantic City, New Jersey. The audience should view both rooms – perhaps the rooms, and stage, are divided exactly, perhaps not. The rooms themselves should be nice, each should have a bed, a desk with a phone, a window with a view, a door to an unseen bathroom and a door to the hall. In short, each should have all the trappings of a modern hotel. Each room is an individual playing area for the actors. The rooms should be almost identical, but they should be mirror images.)

*(The door to Max's room opens and in comes **MAX**, 30s. **MAX** is a buzz-saw and a pro. **MAX** dumps a hand full of chips on the bed, checks his watch. He is agitated.)*

*(**FINN** enters his room. **FINN**, 30s, is modestly dressed and has a distinctive Trotsky mustache.)*

*(**FINN** places a few dollars in his bag, takes a deep breath and then goes to the adjoining door and knocks three times. **MAX** answers the door. **MAX** and **FINN** stare at one another, then **FINN** enters Max's room.)*

FINN. Max, Come on. I...

*(**MAX** throws up his hands.)*

FINN. Oh, the theatrics. I just don't see what the big deal is.

MAX. Whatever. But, *so you know,* you just don't walk away from the table like that. Okay? Not when you haven't crapped out...it's Phil Collins bad.

---

* Please see Music Use Note on page 3.

FINN. *Maybe* Bryan Adams…

MAX. Solo Phil Collins…"No Jacket Required."

FINN. Low blow. Look, I forgot. I was only down on the floor to find you. I just arrived…I only played because you were there.

MAX. The entire table was betting on you…and you were coming through…and then you took your ball and went home. The next guy crapped out on the come out roll. You went from a winner to the gooch…the cooler…It's a common courtesy is all.

FINN. Common courtesy? At a sleazy casino? Please.

MAX. This is not a sleazy casino. This is the Borgata. What you did was bad luck. And what was with your piss ant bets?

FINN. I'm hypoglycemic…I felt weak.

MAX. You felt weak?

FINN. I worked last night. I took the bus down here…I sat next to a woman with an eye-patch, and I'm pretty sure, a dirty diaper. I took two steps off the boardwalk and I thought I was…I don't know where.

MAX. I know, Tyler Perry Presents the end of the fucking world, out there – but not in here…

FINN. So, give me a break.

MAX. Okay. But…I'm gonna need your best Mick Jagger.

FINN. What? No.

MAX. You know the rules. Anywhere, anytime.

FINN. I…No. You want a little…Jag?

(FINN *does a half-assed Mick Jagger impersonation.*)

MAX. Fuck you.

(FINN *does his best Mick Jagger impersonation, perhaps he sings "She's So Cold."* This old routine from college cracks MAX up.)

You still got it. Now. Now. It's over. Onward and upward.

FINN. Thank God. How do you remember this stuff?

---

*Please see Music Use Note on page 3.

(They hug like old friends.)

MAX. I love *this* feeling. This. Anticipation. What is gonna happen? A whole new city to exploit...my best friend. Can you hear them? *(chanting, a la a stadium crowd:)* Finn! Finn! Finn!

FINN. What's in the cards?

MAX. No. What's in the dice. Gotta tell you, despite being completely worthless at the craps table, I'm happy to see you. Oh, I found some old rolls of film and I had them developed.

(MAX goes to his bag and takes out a sleeve of photos, he tosses them to FINN, who flips through them.)

FINN. Who are these people?

MAX. Ahh, that's us.

FINN. Jesus. You look like Tom Cruise in "Cocktail." Am I wearing a poncho?

MAX. The year was 1995 and the hippie harmony of Rusted Root had swept the nation.

FINN. Fuck, we were babies. I remember these girls...12th floor girls.

MAX. Life was good.

FINN. It was...different.

MAX. Are you kidding me? In the ass is different. Those were...some of the best times.

(examining FINN)

And look at you now. Nice taint brush.

FINN. What?

MAX. What's with the facial hair?

(FINN drops the sleeve of photos on the bed.)

FINN. You don't like the Trotsky? Just something new.

MAX. No offense, but you kinda look like an asshole. I mean your mouth...

FINN. I see, my mouth looks like an asshole...how does one not take offense to that?

MAX. It just looks like you should be rolling your own cigarettes and blogging in a coffee shop somewhere... talking about how much you love Amsterdam.

FINN. I like it. You're scared of it. You can touch it.

MAX. Jesus, are you a soccer fan, now? I guess you can pull that shit off in school. I'd get fired.

FINN. It's not night school. It's Columbia...I'm getting my PhD.

MAX. I can't believe they are going to let you teach young people. What's happened to this country?

FINN. Teach? Please. I'm going to be an English professor. I'll profess things to students.

MAX. Ahh. Little will they know what lurks deep in the mind of Dr. Buchanan.

FINN. What's that?

MAX. Oh, Mr. Hyde...of course. Bwhahaha....

(MAX *exits to his bathroom, where he starts the process of getting ready for the evening. Throughout the first scene* MAX *will be in various stages of undress and dress, preparing for a big night out.*)

FINN. Not much lurks there anymore, to tell you the truth. I'm sorry I missed you in New York last time...it was a crazy *(unsaid "time")*.

(MAX *returns, having washed his face.*)

MAX. No worries. It was just a quick trip...for work. It sucked not seeing you, but...I'm just happy we're doing one of these again.

FINN. Yeah.

MAX. I wasn't sure it'd happen. Been a year...fourteen months. Fucking Miami. That was...Wow. I got so drunk I made out with that blind girl.

FINN. I'd forgotten.

MAX. She was good with her hands. Read me like braille. My balls...

FINN. ...Stop...

(**MAX** *mimes braille or the cupping of balls. They share a laugh, it fades.*)

I'm sorry it's been so...It's just...life.

MAX. Life.

(**MAX** *gets a drink.*)

FINN. There's something I want to talk to you about.

MAX. *(distracted)* Speaking of life, my mom died.

FINN. What? Jesus. I thought she was doing okay.

MAX. Was. It ah...Almost five years to the day since her lumpectomy. It was quick.

FINN. When?

MAX. A week ago. I basically came straight here from...

FINN. Fuck, Max. Jesus. I'm sorry. I'm so sorry.

MAX. Don't be. She was a real...what's the word? A bitch. She was a real bitch. One of those people that was only nice to strangers. But she was my mother.

FINN. Are you okay?

MAX. I'm good as gold. Have you ever been to Omaha? That's where she lives...Lived. Omaha, home of Campbell's soup and...? She was laying in this hospital in Omaha...With her latest, and perhaps stupidest boyfriend, Todd, at her bedside...Todd of the trucking industry, Todd of the mustache. She was laying there... My mom. She was there, then she wasn't.

FINN. How's your dad?

MAX. I e-mailed him. It bounced back.

FINN. I don't know what to say.

MAX. That fucking....

(**MAX** *lights a cigarette.*)

FINN. Why didn't you tell me?

MAX. Did you want me to shout it across the craps table?

FINN. Before now, I mean. We could've canceled this weekend.

MAX. Cancel? Are you fucking kidding me? Now more than ever.

FINN. But?

MAX. I don't want to talk about it. Otherwise, everything is…fine.

FINN. Max?

MAX. Good. As. Gold. We should hit this club Murmur tonight, it's ladies' night. But, you can't go out looking like that.

(MAX *enters* FINN*'s room, checking it out.* FINN *is suddenly self-conscious about his clothes.*)

FINN. What's wrong with my clothes?

(As FINN *scurries to catch up,* MAX, *owner of every room he's in, goes through* FINN*'s luggage. He finds a book.*)

MAX. "The Essays of John Dos Pasos?" You plan on reading?

(MAX *finds a packed lunch, he goes through it.*)

You packed your own lunch? In Atlantic City? Home of never-ending buffets. Pudding? Are *you* okay? You have nothing to wear. Jesus, it's like L.L. Bean puked in your bag. Are there suede patches on your underwear?

FINN. I don't take fashion advice from guys that live in San Diego. It's Richard Marx bad.

MAX. Not fair. I do miss New York…San Diego is like living in a post card. Pretty but flat – fucking cardboard. It's not New York…New York…New York girls. Jesus, I miss them…This time of year. After the long winter… the first day the dresses come out and their bodies can be seen…and they know it, God, do they know it. It should be a national holiday. The day the girls bloom like flowers. Blooming day. See, the girls in California have the bodies but that's it…fake tits, fake brains, shaved pussies…Even the ugliest girl in New York has style…carries herself that way…like they're Audrey Hepburn…just a field of Holly Golightlys. Just a little black dress and a smile.

FINN. "*A field of Holly Golightlys?*" You're a real Lord Byron, you know that.

MAX. Lord Byron. He played for the Lakers, right?

FINN. No. He...

(MAX *flips* FINN *the bird.*)

MAX. I miss it. New York girls and you...

FINN. I hardly recognize New York and I live there. It's changed. Look...

(MAX *examining the two rooms.*)

MAX. Do you like the adjoining rooms? Not bad right? Hayden Hall all over. You still keep in touch with that loser from down the hall?

FINN. Ronnie? He's a copy editor for Slate.

MAX. Surprised he could get off the couch long enough to get a job. I thought Peter Tosh's bones were buried in his dorm room....

FINN. He doesn't smoke anymore.

MAX. Good for pothead Ronnie. Never liked that guy.

FINN. I know.

MAX. Always smelled like patchouli and hot pockets.

FINN. Yeah. Do you keep in touch with anybody?

MAX. You. I keep in touch with you. Fuck, I'm on the road two hundred and fifty days a year bribing...I'm sorry... selling doctors these drugs. Let's have a good time. It's a wake up call. You gotta live, have fun, because we all end up in a hospital bed in Omaha one day.

FINN. I...I can't stop thinking about your mom. She'd always come to town and take us to dinner...

MAX. Can we just not? I came here for a reason...to forget...No! To remember the good stuff...

FINN. That reminds me.

(FINN *goes to his room and retrieves a vinyl album from his luggage, The Pixies' iconic "Doolittle." Returning,* FINN *hands it to* MAX.)

For you. For your collection.

MAX. Ah. "Doolittle." This got me through some tough times.

FINN. You said you scratched yours. So, I thought...

MAX. *(earnestly)* Thank you.

FINN. Do you like it? It only cost four bucks. I've never been good at giving gifts, I think it's because my mother got me a subscription to *The New Yorker* when I was six.

MAX. How is Jean?

FINN. You can't spell smother without mother. The curse of the single mom. The "Munch Box" closed.

MAX. The Munch Box?

FINN. Her restaurant. It opened a year ago...closed this winter.

MAX. The Munch Box? It was called "The Munch Box?" No wonder it went under, sounds like a fucking lesbian bar.

FINN. She just keeps saying, "At least I have my health."

(Awkward moment. **MAX** *goes to the mini-bar and starts to sort through all the miniature booze bottles and expensive chips.)*

MAX. What's this shit you told me about not writing anymore?

FINN. Same thing I told you the last time you asked.

MAX. What about the book? The book...the memoir you wanted to write about all the girls you've slept with?

FINN. "52 Pick Up."

MAX. Yes. 52 different girls..."52 Pick Up." Genius.

FINN. It was a terrible idea.

MAX. I liked your shit. The short stories and whatever...I dug those plays.

FINN. I was just another asshole from Connecticut writing plays set in West Texas.

MAX. They were good.

FINN. They weren't plays, Max, they were just mundane observations. I wrote a play titled, "People Talk Fast." It was three hours long...

MAX. So what?

FINN. So, it wasn't a play, it was a hostage situation.

MAX. You know what you should write? Graphic novels. They sell like hotcakes, and they're making movies out of them left and right.

FINN. Graphic novels? Novels? I love that…THEY ARE FUCKING COMIC BOOKS.

MAX. Forget it.

FINN. If you want to be considered literature, try not having characters that can FLY. Perhaps don't draw the stories…

MAX. Don't start. It's a shame, telling girls you're a writer was a real panty dropper. You'll come back to it.

*(**FINN** notices that **MAX** has opened some peanuts from the mini bar or hospitality basket. **FINN** reads from the list of prices for the snacks.)*

FINN. Why did you do that? Those are sixteen dollar peanuts.

*(**MAX** just smiles and continues to munch.)*

You know, I was reading some of the pamphlets in my room. I was thinking about checking out the Atlantic City Historical Society.

MAX. The Historical Society?

FINN. It's free. It says that the Historical Society has 20,000 artifacts that illustrate the county's major 19th-century shipbuilding industry. I was surprised, there are some pretty good shows this weekend. There's this ventriloquist.

MAX. Oh.

*(**MAX** examines the pamphlet, then playfully humps it on the bed.)*

Wow. This is fun. Let's flip this bitch over.

(He flips the pamphlet over, still humping it, then continues.)

MAX. I have a better idea. Let's actually go have fun. If the lobby is any indication, there's some serious strange in this hotel.

FINN. Yeah. I saw three bachelorette parties when I checked in.

MAX. Ah, the bachelorettes. Like wounded animals on the Serengeti during feeding time. Doomed. Did I mention ladies night? Start here, maybe find some local trim – and then if things look bleak, we can hit the boardwalk. It's going to be epic.

FINN. They're not animals.

MAX. We're all animals. First one to ten wins.

FINN. What?

MAX. That's how we scored it, right?

FINN. Don't ask me.

MAX. Single girls three points – married women five points – right?

FINN. I guess.

MAX. Guess, may ass. Your rules.

FINN. I'm feeling a little under the weather. I have this, ah, tickle – I don't know…I can't afford to let it move into my chest…I just…

(MAX *en route to the bathroom, hands* FINN *the can of peanuts.*)

MAX. Here are some nuts. Sack up.

(MAX *exits into his bathroom.*)

(O.S.) Know who I thought of the other day? Right in the middle of a meeting – burst out laughing thinking about her – my boss thought I was fucking crazy.

(MAX *returns from the bathroom.*)

That girl from Cabo. Do you remember The Shocker? Beware of the Shocker! Bwwwahhhha!

FINN. (*smiling despite himself*) How could I forget? She violated me.

MAX. What did you say? What was it you said to her?

FINN. *Excuse me.*

MAX. That's right. Girl shoves a finger up your ass without warning…I mean, it's one thing if she says, "Do you mind," or maybe, "Get ready," but not a fucking peep. Complete unchecked aggression in my book – I mean, she is knuckle deep in your ass and *you* say, "Excuse me," like she cut in line waiting for the movies.

FINN. What does one say?

MAX. You say "get your finger out of my ass, bitch."

FINN. That was the intent.

MAX. You've always been too polite, Finn, that's why you never get what you want.

(MAX finds and orders pay-per-view porn on his television.)

(The grunts and screams of porno sex emanate from the TV.)

FINN. Are you watching porn?

MAX. Yes, but only for the articles.

FINN. Why?

MAX. Because I want to. Kids today with the internet porn, the short attention spans – they just get the big finish – but they miss the storytelling. For instance, this is a tragic story about a housewife stuck in a loveless marriage.

FINN. Ah, a classic. Like Madame Bovary.

MAX. Sure. Whatever.

(They watch the porn for a moment. Breaking from the trance…)

FINN. This is…I don't know what.

(FINN turns off the television.)

Max, before this goes any further.

(MAX gets on the floor and starts to do sit ups or push ups.)

MAX. Are you ready to gamble? No bullshit this time.

FINN. The truth be told. I, ah. Listen to me.

MAX. What? What now? Please don't get all...whatever on me.

FINN. I really can't gamble, Max.

MAX. Fuck you. I told you I got the rooms...

FINN. Thank you...but...

MAX. But, what?

FINN. I don't have any money. Hell, I shouldn't even be down here...I'm flat broke.

MAX. Are you fucking kidding me?

FINN. I'm sorry, man. It all came crashing down last week... I had half a mind to cancel the whole weekend, but you seemed so...you made the reservation already... I'm not even sure where I'm getting the money for school.

(MAX *stops exercising.*)

MAX. What's up?

FINN. I fucked up...My mother's restaurant. It was just... She thought it was just a dip. I bailed her out...She said she'd pay me back.

MAX. You didn't. Oh no. You didn't...You put money into the Munch Box!? The Munch Box? No.

FINN. It's gone. The university doesn't pay shit. Even with the scholarships...I'm short. My credit is shot. I tried to get a private loan, but the banks aren't lending. The fucking economy. I don't know.

MAX. Then what?

FINN. I'll have to take a year off or...it's a fucking disaster.

MAX. Fuck.

FINN. I don't know...I just don't know...

MAX. How much do you need?

FINN. Max, it doesn't matter. I should have just...

MAX. How much?

FINN. Really?

MAX. I don't have any fucking kids to support here.... You're my friend. How much?

FINN. Ten grand.

MAX. That's it? You don't need more? You, my friend, are the first recipient of the Max Emerson Scholarship for...what? Old idiot friends and their mothers. I'll even give you some pocket money for the powder room.

(MAX finds the can of nuts and tosses the can to FINN.)

FINN. No way. I. You don't have to...

MAX. That's done, okay? All of it...Stop thinking about it. Now, I'm going to shit-shower-shave. Then let's hit the floor...

FINN. Max, I don't know what to say.

(They hug.)

MAX. Shh. This is nice. Okay. It's over. We're going to burn Atlantic City to the ground. I have us all sorted out. *(beat)* I have coke; do you want some coke?

FINN. It's 4:30 in the afternoon.

MAX. You're right. Not till after five...is that a rule? Do you know how hard it is to score coke in AC?

FINN. No.

MAX. Hard. I had to call this old client of mine, that's ironic being a drug rep...fuck you Pfizer. Anyway, the guy would only sell in bulk...

(MAX retrieves his cocaine which is hidden away. He makes a theatrical presentation of the absurdly large package.)

Please don't be shy...

FINN. *(stunned)* It looks like a burrito.

(MAX exits into the bathroom, but continues the conversation.)

FINN. Look there's something else I need to talk to you about.

MAX. *(O.S.)* I did some research. No fully-nude clubs in this town. Only bikini bars...bullshit, right? A town full of casinos and filth, but no fully nude strip clubs? Can you believe that?

(**MAX** *returns, toothbrush in hand.*)

Call room service…get whatever you want – it's on me.

(**MAX** *returns to his shower.*)

FINN. Thanks…and thanks.

(*A moment passes.* **FINN** *looks at the room and looks at the coke, taking it all in. He gingerly places the cocaine down and goes to the mini-bar and opens it, peering inside he takes out a beer, thinks better of it, returns it and takes out a can of soda. He looks at the sheet that has the cost of the soda on it, and laughs to himself. He sits in a chair and pops it open. A moment later he pulls out his cell phone. He dials a number…it rings once, it rings twice…then* **FINN** *hangs up the phone. A second later his phone rings, he answers.*)

Hello? Hey babe. No. I don't think I did. Did I? Just now. Really? I guess it must've dialed you in my pocket. Just, yeah. Hanging out. You won't believe this but Max offered…Okay. Then go ahead and get back to work, I don't want to get you in trouble. I love you too.

(*He hangs up. He sips his soda.* **MAX** *returns fresh from the shower wearing only boxers.*)

MAX. Did you get yourself a soda, kiddo? You wanna turn around or something? Hey look, its snowing.

(**MAX** *starts to powder his nether regions with talcum powder.* **FINN** *turns his back to* **MAX**.)

I just thought of that girl Ashley. The one we shared in Vegas.

FINN. You told her I was a podiatrist. I spent half the night examining her arches.

MAX. Jesus, it was like sticking my dick in a beehive.

FINN. Desperate times call for desperate measures.

MAX. Desperate is right…She was something else. If you add it up. How many times?

FINN. How many times?

MAX. Have I gotten you laid?

FINN. You? Fuck you. I can do...I have done okay on my own, thank you very much. Pulled my weight. You're getting senile in your old age.

MAX. A real swinging dick, huh? Let's settle this once and for all. Come on. Let's see it. Winner buys dinner.

FINN. What are you...?

MAX. Wait. Length or girth? Both?

FINN. Are you serious?

MAX. Come on. I'll call the front desk and get a ruler. Not enough room? Yard stick? Should I open the door?

FINN. Fuck you. I'm not...

MAX. *(laughing)* The look on your face. I'll buy dinner anyway.

FINN. No. Just put some fucking pants on.

MAX. I insist. What time is it?

FINN. *(checking)* Five minutes since the last time you asked.

MAX. Close enough. Time to stop, drop and roll...

(MAX *finds his drugs and starts to cut up some lines. He rolls up a dollar bill.*)

FINN. Really?

MAX. I seem to remember last time you were a hoover. There was never enough. Like a fucking anteater.

(MAX *snorts a line.*)

Sweet Jesus, I'm home. The shampoo effect.

FINN. *(remembering)* Wash, rinse, repeat.

(MAX *snorts another line. He offers* FINN *the bill.*)

MAX. Your turn.

FINN. No, thank you. Look, Max there's...

MAX. Why don't you go shower?

FINN. Listen man...

MAX. You can borrow a shirt. Because you aren't getting laid looking like that...unless we happen upon a meeting of young homosexual communists. Maybe not even then.

FINN. Are you listening?

MAX. Yes, Finn. Yes. I'm listening.

FINN. I'm going to have a baby.

(silence)

MAX. Odd. You're not even showing. With a girl?

FINN. Yeah, with a girl.

MAX. Your first time?

FINN. What do you mean?

MAX. You must've? At some point before... All the...? It's not the first time you've gotten a girl pregnant, is it?

FINN. Yes.

MAX. Oh boy, you're in it now, boy...It happened to me once. It happens to the best of us.

FINN. When?

MAX. Before. Does it matter?

FINN. This is different.

MAX. I don't think it is.

FINN. This isn't a one night stand.

MAX. Oh, you two are together?

FINN. We're having a baby.

MAX. *We're* having a baby? Me and you? Are you going to make an honest man out of me?

FINN. I don't know, is that possible?

(an awkward hesitation)

MAX. So...?

FINN. So...she's due in the fall.

MAX. Wow. I guess we both came baring news, huh?

FINN. *(a look)*

MAX. Well. Congratulations are in order, I guess. Congratulations. Tell me...who's the proud mama?

FINN. Her name is Susan. Susan Poland.

MAX. Wait, Susan Poland? Not NYU Susan?

FINN. The same.

MAX. Holy shit, the actress? I remember her. I remember her.

FINN. Oh yeah?

MAX. Yeah. I think I fucked her. *(beat)* I'm just kidding.

FINN. You prick. We reconnected a while ago and...started talking...It's funny actually...

MAX. Is it?

FINN. Is it what?

MAX. Is it funny?

FINN. I mean in the ironic...

MAX. ...You always had a thing for her. Good for you. Really? An actress?

FINN. Former.

MAX. A former writer and a former actress... Jesus the Boulevard of Broken Dreams. Remember that girl, Julie? She was an actress and she was a real bunny boiler. She hid in my closet.

FINN. That Julie girl wasn't an actress, she did burlesque.

MAX. What's wrong with burlesque? It's the best thing to happen to fat chicks since black guys.

FINN. *(ignoring the last remark)* Susan is back at school. That's where we met again. She's studying Social Policy.

MAX. Oh my God...good for her. For you. Good for her and you. This calls for a celebration, or at least a drowning of sorrows. Let's talk about it over some cocktails.

FINN. Yeah. Drinks are fine, talking is fine...but I don't want to...ah...

(MAX *stands, going toward the door.*)

MAX. It's a wonder you quit writing, you're so fucking articulate.

FINN. I don't want to spend the whole night chasing women.

(MAX *stops.*)

MAX. What are you talking about?

FINN. Not like before. I can't. With the baby and all...Just so we're on the same page.

MAX. The hits just keep on coming with you…You're killing me here. It's just us.

FINN. Max. Look. I know. But everything has changed.

MAX. It doesn't have to. Your secret is safe with me, Finn. Let's go. This is our weekend, right? Everything is confidential.

FINN. I don't want to lie to her.

MAX. You know my philosophy…there's absolutely nothing honest about monogamy. Monogamy is about repressing every urge a person has…your complete nature. It is the essence of lying to oneself. I tell you man, it's in our blood…our particles…

FINN. Here we go, I've heard this speech a thousand times…

MAX. Not like this. We're all so fucking small. Don't you get it? We are these tiny insignificant blobs of banded together protein, sitting on some dirt in the midst of a universe which is probably just a white hole piggy-backed on a black hole.

FINN. What is this?

MAX. I have cable, I'm not an idiot. My point is…

FINN. You have a point…?

MAX. My point is, asshole, my point is…don't try to deny yourself, because you can't. What are the two things that we, as humans, try over and over again to attain, but never can? Peace and monogamy. Fighting and fucking. Fighting and fucking. We can't help ourselves. It is who we are. Humans don't mate for life. It is a scientific fact. We tell ourselves we do, but it's a lie society forces on us…Because deep down – so far down – in the smallest darkest part of us – we know that if do, we'll go extinct. Let the Wolves and Pandas that are too dumb to screw walk off into the species sunset. But not us…Our life force screams for us to protect and produce. Protect and produce. It's bigger than us. Everything is bigger than us.

FINN. Have you ever considered that perhaps you're a sex addict?

MAX. Oh. I love that modern diagnosis...Do you know what a sex addict is? A man. A fucking man. Every man in life – fathers, uncles, heroes and priests – every man in history...Ghandi was a womanizer, Martin Luther King, even Christ hung out with a hooker – and it wasn't for the conversation...

FINN. Stop. You don't understand...you won't understand how it feels...

MAX. Don't look down your nose at me just because you knocked some chick up.

FINN. I have fucked around on every girl I've ever gone out with. Fucked up every relationship. I'm trying to evolve here.

MAX. Oh, I get it. Finn is all grow'd up.

FINN. I don't want anymore blind spots in my life. We aren't kids anymore.

MAX. That's all relative.

FINN. No, it's not. It's the opposite of relative. It is quantitative. I mean, don't you ever feel life creeping in?

MAX. Did you have a mid-life crisis?

FINN. A whole-life crisis. I have lost that gear...I can't reach that speed anymore...I sit up at night and think, fuck...I've done nothing with my life. But...Susan... this baby is something. A real something – it's gonna be flesh and bone and...And it's not just the baby...it's Susan...She and I – us – is something too. She cares about odd numbers. She told me that when she was a little girl, she felt that even numbers got too much attention...2,4,6,8...

MAX. I know what even numbers are!

FINN. Okay. Susan thought that even numbers had lots of friends...so she cared – had feelings for – the odd numbers. She has compassion for the world...and I envy it. I love it. I love her. I do. You should be happy for me.

MAX. I just stuck my mother in the ground.

FINN. I'm sorry. I just...you know, we can still have fun.

MAX. Oh yeah, it'll be great. Maybe we can knock back a few Shirley Temples...oohh, I know, lets go see the boat show at the Atlantic City Historical Society.

FINN. *(to himself)* It's not a boat show, it's a show about the county's major 19th-century industry...shipbuilding.

MAX. Shut up. I'm really disappointed. Pretty soon, we'll be there.

FINN. Where?

MAX. You know...*there*. We're going to start swapping recipes and visiting the wine country. Before you know it, we're that guy – that fucking guy – with the plaid shirt and the fucking Birkenstock sandals *with socks* and the scratched Pixies albums. Some fat asshole who denies every impulse he has...

FINN. It doesn't have to be that way.

MAX. We're on our way...before we know it, the only thing that makes us individuals is going to be our *oh so* clever e-mail addresses...

FINN. Come on...

MAX. ...I think "Hamlet2 at gmail" says something about me...

FINN. That won't happen. Come on. You know I hate e-mail. As though they're letters..."L-O-L". What does that mean? *(beat)* Virginia Woolf, Vaclav Havel...Those are letters...

MAX. Don't you dare! Don't you fucking dare bring that pretentious grad school shit into this room when there is bigger shit going on. We said we were going to *always* do it this way. A couple of days where we can be every terrible wonderful thing we actually are.

FINN. What do you want to hear? That I still desire?

MAX. Sure.

FINN. I still desire. I still see other women and think...I see the legions of girls with yoga mats rolled up sooo tight. Where are they going? But, you know, there is an Indian saying, Max. It goes like this: "It is morning when you wake up."

MAX. What the fuck? Did you get that out of a fortune cookie?

FINN. Indian, Max, Indian. We had a points system. We made women into statistics.

MAX. What? And they don't have statistics on us? How much we make? Where we went to school? The size of our dicks? Shall I go on? They read us like the back of baseball cards. You don't think that Susan checked your stats before...

FINN. Maybe. But she didn't go around jumping in and out of bed – then keeping score.

MAX. Who knows, maybe she did?

FINN. Shut up. That's my...What does that even mean?

MAX. Nothing. How many guys did she tell you she slept with? Hmm? Let me guess...Four? Right? *(ticking them off)* High School boyfriend. College boyfriend. One mistake and...you?

FINN. *(a look)*

(FINN retreats to his room.)

MAX. More importantly...more importantly does Susan know about all our little adventures? Did you let her know?

FINN. Well...

MAX. Come on you must've told her about our...

FINN. ...I...

MAX. ...Honest Abe...Joe-fucking-life-change – you must've?

FINN. Yes. I did. We tell each other...everything...

MAX. You told her what these weekends are about? Let me see your cell.

FINN. Why?

MAX. Just let me see it.

FINN. No.

MAX. I just want to see a picture of Susan. It has been a decade. I bet you have a current picture of Susan on your phone. I want to see what she looks like.

FINN. Fine.

(FINN *takes out his cell phone and flips through a few pictures. Eventually finding one.*)

Here.

(*He holds the phone timidly toward* MAX.)

MAX. Closer.

FINN. No.

MAX. I can't see it. I'm not going to bite.

(FINN *inches closer. When he does,* MAX *pounces on the phone he holds in close to himself, then far away as* FINN *tries to regain control of it. A chase ensues, it leads from room to room. A childish pursuit.*)

Oh, she looks great, Finn. Really.

FINN. (*nonchalant*) Give it back.

MAX. Should I call her? I'm dialing…

FINN. Ha ha. Very funny.

MAX. …It's ringing!…

FINN. Be careful! Did you just push a button?

MAX. Hello? Susan. Max Emerson here…remember me from college? OF COURSE YOU DO, you called me *Maximum Overdrive.*

FINN. You didn't call her. Please don't call her!

(*Soon* MAX *has retreated to standing on the bed.*)

MAX. (*affected*) Me and Finn, we take these little vacations. But instead of playing golf and eating at shitty steak houses we screw girls…lots and lots of girls – black ones, white ones, yellow ones – fat-skinny – polka-dotted – all of them. Yep, we screw them and we're usually too drunk and high to remember. Great. I'll let him know.

(MAX *hangs up the phone.*)

FINN. You didn't call her.

MAX. Maybe, maybe not. Does it matter? I thought you said she knew?

FINN. You wouldn't call her?

(MAX *drops the phone on the bed.* FINN *looks at it and then absentmindedly leaves it there.*)

MAX. I was making a point...

FINN. A point?!

MAX. You're already lying to her. And the thing is, you're going to miss it. Everything we had, the things we were able to do...

(FINN *exits into his room, leaving his phone on* MAX's *bed.* FINN *gathers his things as* MAX *lingers at the adjoining door.*)

Stop. If we don't leave soon we are going to miss the happy hour.

FINN. I don't care.

MAX. Don't pout. I'll buy you a milk shake.

FINN. This...this is obviously not going to work. We've changed. I've moved on and you haven't. I should just go home.

MAX. So I should just send you the check? Money order?

FINN. Um. Well. I mean...

MAX. That's what you came here for. Did Sue send you down here to get the money?

FINN. No. She's working two fucking jobs...she...you don't even know her. You know, ever since I first met you, I've done everything you wanted. Everything that you've wanted to try or...endless nights...going to the Wetlands and Mercury Lounge every night...all those dumb girls...Party Girl Pootie, Sally from the Valley, Lindsey whatsherfuck, Sarah Berger...fucking Sam...

MAX. Sam?

FINN. Blonde, big tits.

MAX. Sam! Oh, Sam...I miss Sam.

FINN. Hanging out at The Blue and Gold till dawn the night before mid-terms...

MAX. How much fun was that?

FINN. I got a C-plus! Do you remember in college that I even dumped a girl I liked because...

MAX. This again? Larry Legend?

FINN. ...You were heartbroken so I had to be single with you. You manipulate...

MAX. You're not married to this woman!

FINN. Yes, I am!

(silence)

MAX. What? Metaphorically?

FINN. No. I'm already married. Susan and I got married two months ago...

MAX. What?

FINN. I was going to tell you...

MAX. What? Really, Finn? That...that...just...ouch.

FINN. I was going...I went down to the floor to tell you.

MAX. Two months? I was *in* New York two months ago.

FINN. I know it's old fashioned but I wanted to do the right thing. Be there, unlike our fathers.

MAX. Our fathers understood. You. You. You have serious balls.

FINN. I'm sorry, Max.

MAX. You have the audacity – the fucking audacity – to borrow *ten thousand dollars* and then spring all this shit on me? "Arms for the poor."

FINN. It's ALMS for the poor...not arms. The poor have arms, presumably.

MAX. This is bad...this is fucking Billy Joel bad....fuck you.

FINN. I just knew you'd freak at the whole idea. You hate...

MAX. You didn't want me at your fucking wedding?

FINN. Max.

MAX. Not *in* your wedding…but *at* your wedding? You couldn't even tell me? A fucking phone call. Wait. Who was your best man?

FINN. I. Does it…? I didn't think, you'd want…

MAX. Wait.

FINN. 'Cause I didn't want to hear this shit, man..

MAX. No. No.

FINN. You're hard…I could hear it coming a mile away…

MAX. *(realizing)* NO! Pothead Ronnie?! Pothead fucking Ronnie?

FINN. Max, things change…and…I'm sorry but they have, they just have.

MAX. Pothead Ronnie? Fuck you.

FINN. I. Max. I.

(A sad silence. **FINN** *with nothing left to say.)*

MAX. Well, fuck you. Fuck you dead.

(Silence. **MAX** *retreats into his room, slamming the adjoining door.* **FINN** *sits on his bed, his head falling into his hands.)*

(In **MAX**'s *room,* **MAX** *fumes – punching the air in fury. He settles himself and does a couple of lines of coke, then a couple more. He sees* **FINN**'s *cell phone still on the bed. He picks up* **FINN**'s *phone and stares at it.)*

(In **FINN**'s *room, he realizes he does not have his phone.* **FINN** *goes to the adjoining door and knocks.)*

FINN. Max. Look, man, can I have my phone?

(In **MAX**'s *room,* **MAX** *puts the phone in his pocket, does another bump and exits into the hall.* **FINN** *knocks.)*

Look man, I'm sorry. But, I need my phone. I just want to go home and we can talk about this shit later…

*(***FINN** *opens the door and goes into* **MAX**'s *room. He looks around, sees* **MAX** *is nowhere to be found. He searches for his phone, but can't find it. He becomes more and more frantic while searching.)*

FINN. *(cont.)* Where are you, where are you...

(FINN uses the room phone to call his phone. MAX answers.)

Max...It's Finn, who do you think it is? I need my phone. Max...I know. I know. Look look look...Please don't call Susan. Please. I'm sorry. I...I...PLEASE. *(beat)* Hello?

(MAX has hung up.)

Fuck me.

(FINN looks around, his world falling apart. He opens the mini-bar and grabs a beer. He cracks it and drinks deep. It quenches something.)

FUCK!

(A slow fade. The Pixies "Caribou" blares into a full black out.*)

---

*Please see Music Use Note on Page 3.

Scene Two
"TERMINAL Or The Hard Way"

(Both rooms are half-lit.)

(In FINN's room, we find FINN passed out on his bed. Surrounding FINN are a couple of beer cans and a book, it is obvious that FINN has been drinking and reading.)

(In MAX's room, we find MAX sitting on the end of his bed smoking, he plays with some dice half-heartedly.)

(MAX makes a decision and enters FINN's room in a flurry. He leaves the adjoining door wide open.)

(MAX sees FINN asleep and is soon attacking him with a pillow.)

MAX. TERRORIST ATTACK! 9/11! 9/11!

FINN. Who are you?

MAX. I'm Peter Pan.

FINN. I just shut my eyes. Just my eyes. I was dreaming...I was in a castle and I had to defend it from this fog. It was impossible.

MAX. This isn't a dream.

(MAX does a bump of coke off his hand or keys.)

FINN. Shouldn't you detox.

MAX. I don't detox. I tox.

FINN. Why didn't you answer my calls? I called. You didn't call Susan, did you?

MAX. That's what you want to talk about? There are more important things, don't you think? Don't you have something to say to me?

FINN. Did you?

MAX. You're not listening. That doesn't matter. Look, I've been thinking. I've come to the conclusion – the realization – that I would never have let you down the way you...But friends forgive and forget. Forgive and forget. Right? I think I can find a way to forgive you.

FINN. Forgive me?

MAX. Yes, because I'm not a woman, like yourself. I have a dick. If I were a woman...this whole wedding thing... the fucking betrayal with...God help you if I were a woman. Shit if I were my mother...hell hath no fury.

FINN. Max. Look, man you hate weddings...how many times...

MAX. I'll forgive you. But, you have to say you're sorry first.

FINN. Fuck you, man.

MAX. Fuck me? That hurt, what you did. Say you're sorry.

FINN. I admit, I regret...

MAX. Fuck your regret. Say: I, Finn Buchanan, being of sound mind and body, apologize for being a backstabbing, manipulative and greedy little shit of man....with a stupid fucking mustache.

FINN. I'm not saying that.

MAX. Fuck you. Say it.

FINN. I...

(MAX *continues to pummel* FINN *with the pillow.*)

MAX. Fuck you. Say it.

FINN. Okay. Okay. How does it start?

(MAX *helps* FINN *stumble through...*)

I, Finn Buchanan, being of sound mind and body... apologize for being a backstabbing...and manipulative, greedy little shit of man...with a stupid fucking mustache.

MAX. Let the healing begin.

(MAX *tosses* FINN *his phone.*)

FINN. Thank you. Thank you.

MAX. Susan does have compassion, you're right. You can hear it in her voice.

FINN. You didn't.

MAX. She's practically my sister-in-law, I think I can call her if I want. Do you know she remembers me, from school? I mentioned you were up big on the floor. Told her how you bet ten the hard way and it hit. That you were way up. Who knows? Maybe ten thousand dollars big? Don't make me a liar.

FINN. What?

MAX. You heard me.

FINN. Oh, like before? Bullshit. She didn't ask you why you had my phone?

(FINN *checks the phone's call log.*)

Holy shit. You actually called her. What did you tell her?!

MAX. I told her you couldn't talk on the phone at the tables. She really trusts you, you're probably right... don't want to ruin that by telling the truth.

FINN. You called her. You told her, didn't you! I can't believe you called her. Oh my God. Oh my God.

MAX. She sent you a text message.

Let me see if I can remember...

(*reciting from memory*)

Congrats on your winnings exclamation point. What timing question mark exclamation point. CRAZY. L-O-L. Love S.

(MAX *takes out ten orange thousand dollar chips from his pockets and drops them before* FINN.)

(FINN *is looking at the message, then at the chips.*)

FINN. Those are worth...?

MAX. Ten grand.

(*Overcome with emotion,* FINN *embraces* MAX. *It is a childish rejoice.*)

FINN. I don't know what to say.

MAX. You don't have to say anything. She is a sweet girl. Really.

FINN. Why do you...? I'm going to ask you something. I want you to answer me truthfully. Back in school, did anything go on between you and Susan...back in school?

(**MAX** *lights a cigarette.*)

MAX. Could you repeat the question? I'm a little deaf in this ear.

FINN. You motherfucker. You're just being intentionally daft.

MAX. Am I?

FINN. Yes.

MAX. Daft?

FINN. You know what I mean.

MAX. I do?

FINN. You're doing it right now.

MAX. Really?

FINN. Shut up and answer the question.

MAX. No. I've known you a long time, Finn. You're my friend...I don't have a lot of people that I...I'm sorry if you think I've abused you in some way. I'm sorry if you think I've not come far enough as a person or something. But, I know who I am.

FINN. Max, I don't feel well.

MAX. Because you're sick! I'm going to make you well. First have a drink and a bump.

FINN. What is it you want?

MAX. I want one night.

FINN. One night?

MAX. An all in...swinging for the fences...explosion.

FINN. You just want to party?

MAX. No. I just want to party *with you.*

FINN. With me?

MAX. Yeah. I tell you what though, I refuse...I won't blame...I won't blame you or regret...Look, I'm glad for all the shit I've done. Was it always the right thing? I don't know. Probably not. Sometimes, definitely not. But. BUT. We always had a good time, and nobody got hurt. Let's do this. The time is night.

FINN. The time is nigh. *Nigh.*

(MAX throws up his arms.)

MAX. Are you going to have a good time or what?

(FINN, arms up in surrender.)

FINN. Yes. Yes. Get me a drink for God's sake.

(MAX gets them drinks. FINN is looking at the chips.)

MAX. Think of those chips as a wedding gift. Don't lose them.

(FINN places the chips in his pockets.)

FINN. No chasing girls, right? I'll party – but I don't want to spend tonight chasing ass.

MAX. Even the bachelorettes are fast asleep. That ship has sailed.

FINN. Good.

(MAX raises his glass in a toast.)

MAX. To…to…

FINN. Friends.

(They toast. As they do, MISSY enters from MAX's bathroom. MISSY, attractive, 30s. She looks older than she is, and carries herself in an obviously forced adolescent manner. As though, if she plays the part hard enough, it just might stick. MISSY wears a party dress and her hair is wet from a shower. FINN notices her.)

Max. Max, there is a woman in your room.

MAX. Oh. That's Missy. Hi, Missy.

MISSY. Hi.

MAX. *(to MISSY)* This is the one I was telling you about. Finn, this is the ravishing Missy Aggravation.

FINN. Hello.

MISSY. I feel like a new woman. Getting out of work clothes. Thanks for letting me use the shower, Max. Don't I look better?

MAX. Exquisite.

MISSY. That's good, right?

(MISSY retreats back into MAX's bathroom, drying her hair.)

(During the rest of the play we have two playing areas in the two rooms, allowing for separate scenes to take place simultaneously. The party flows back and forth between the two.)

FINN. Who is that?

MAX. That's Missy.

FINN. Who's Missy?

MAX. Missy is Missy. I met her at the craps table, she wants to party.

FINN. Is she a pro?

MAX. She's a girl.

FINN. We just said no chasing women.

MAX. This isn't chasing. She was already here.

FINN. Semantics? You're a child. Max. You said. I thought. I thought you wanted to party with me?

MAX. I do. It's all party favors.

(MISSY returns from the bathroom.)

MISSY. Do you have more coke?

MAX. Speaking of which. Do we have more coke....I think we do...

(MAX grabs his drugs and cuts out some lines of coke on the Pixies album.)

FINN. Max didn't tell me he had company. I can leave you guys alone.

MAX. Don't you fucking dare. This party is for you.

FINN. My party, I see.

MISSY. I ran into Max at the craps table, and he was burning them up.

MAX. Missy works at the Tropicana.

MISSY. Don't tell anybody, you boys. We aren't supposed to hang out with visitors.

MAX. Don't worry. We're great with secrets.

MISSY. Me too. Ha ha. Where have you been all night, Finn?

FINN. I was here, in hell.

MISSY. You want hell? Go to the boardwalk. This is nice. I tell you, Max was hot at the table tonight, weren't you baby?

MAX. Hotter than hot. I couldn't lose. Didn't matter what I bet. I was rolling it. Fever five. Nina. Easy six. Yo-leven. I was the Patron Saint of Boxcars. Sometimes it comes so easy. Ladies first.

(MAX passes the drugs to MISSY, who snorts a line.)

MISSY. I walked up and said, "Hello, do you want some company?" And look at his eyes, what was I supposed to do? They're so sad...like a kicked puppy.

FINN. That's how he gets you.

(MISSY holds the drugs out toward FINN. FINN stares at the drugs.)

I'll pass.

MAX. If not now, when? Live fast, die young and leave a good looking corpse.

MISSY. You planning on dying soon?

MAX. Touch and go. You never know.

FINN. What does that even mean?

MAX. It means, that these are the moments. Right now. I could be dead in a year, a week, a minute.

MISSY. You're funny, isn't he funny?

MAX. In fact, just to get it out of the way, Finn – so there is no confusion – I'm going to go ahead and invite you to my funeral.

FINN. Fuck you.

MAX. Don't worry. I haven't set a date. But, I need this weekend. I need my friend.

(FINN does a line of coke.)

What did you say? "Morning is when you wake up?" Well, good morning.

FINN. Wow. What's for breakfast?

(They all laugh.)

MAX. We're ahead of you. Catch up.

*(**FINN** snorts another line.)*

FINN. Rusty pipes.

*(**MAX** playfully kisses **MISSY**.)*

Ya know. I really... *(noticing)* Nevermind.

*(**MAX** coming up for air.)*

MAX. What?

FINN. I don't want to bore Missy.

MISSY. Don't worry about me. I got everything I need.

MAX. Say it.

FINN. I just wanted to tell Max here...that I'm sorry. All bullshit aside. I am sorry that I hurt your feelings earlier.

MAX. Oh. We're off of that.

MISSY. Oh, how cute, you guys are like little boys sharing toys.

FINN. I knew at the time what I was doing was...

MISSY. Ooohh. What did he do?

MAX. Nothing. Make yourself a drink.

FINN. What I did was Don Henley bad.

MAX. Stop! Nothing is as bad as Don Henley.

MISSY. I like Don Henley.

(They both stop to register what has been said. Amazed.)

FINN. I had enough questions of my own about what I was doing, without having you in my ear.

MAX. Wait a second. Questions? Did you hear that Missy? Finn has questions.

FINN. I mean, concerns. Worries. I don't know. You know, I spend my life in the library or with Susan. Every minute. It can be...a little much. Now with the baby coming? We live in Park Slope and all I see are these strollers. Thousands of them. I just think, "Fuck. Who the fuck are these people?" I'm these fucking people. I've practically had to amputate everything else.

MAX. Because you don't think you can trust yourself otherwise?

FINN. I didn't say that.

MISSY. No, you didn't.

FINN. Let me ask you. Are you totally happy all the time ever, Max? Missy?

MISSY. Look at me. I'm the happiest person on planet Earth. Ha ha.

MAX. I tell you what you do...You just slip out the back, Jack. Make a new plan, Stan. You don't need to be coy, Roy. Just set yourself free...Finn.

FINN. Not me, I'm not my dad.

MAX. Shit, even if you're perfect they'll still blame you for something, right, Missy?

MISSY. Who?

MAX. Kids.

MISSY. I sure hope not. If my daughter hated me...I don't know what.

FINN. You have a child? That's wonderful. Really.

MAX. You have a kid, huh?

MISSY. *(almost to herself)* Katie.

MAX. No shit? That's my mother's name.

MISSY. Look at it this way, at least you know I put out.

FINN. I realize I don't know anything about kids. That scares me.

MISSY. Nothing to be scared of...

FINN. How do you...? I know they don't sleep.

MISSY. When they're newborns, don't plan on sleeping... my...

FINN. What do they like...?

MAX. What is this? Kids like hot dogs, women like money. Can we quit with the Oxygen Network shit?

MISSY. Kids are like everybody else. They just want to be loved.

MAX. Well, here's to that.

(MAX drinks.)

I'm gonna hit the head, then we can proceed to get pinned and solve the world's problems.

(MAX exits to the bathroom. FINN feels the drugs, examines his situation.)

FINN. *(singing the Pixies' Gouge Away to himself)* "Missy Aggravation. Some Sacred questions. You stroke my locks…" Legs? Is that what he says?

(MISSY laughs.)

MISSY. So, you're from New York, huh?

(There is a knock at the door. FINN looks surprised.)

She made it.

FINN. I'm sorry? She?

(MISSY goes to the door and VICTORIA enters. VICTORIA is pretty, if a bit naive; perhaps in over her head. She wears a dress and a smile.)

MISSY. My girl.

(The girls hug.)

VICTORIA. Missy. I found it. This is way off the boardwalk.

FINN. Max? There is another she here.

(MAX returns from the bathroom.)

MAX. Well, well, well. Twice as nice. Now we're even.

FINN. Max.

MISSY. *(to MAX)* Didn't I tell you she was pretty?

(to FINN)

Max said he had a friend, so I said I have a friend too…

FINN. And what a friend it is.

MAX. I'm sorry, and this Ferrari's name is…?

VICTORIA. Victoria.

MAX. As in Crown Vic. Sorry. Wrong car.

MISSY. Did you hear what he said. You're funny, Max. Isn't he funny?

FINN. Hilarious. Max?

MAX. Victoria, this is the dark man himself, Mr. Hyde. It's his party.

FINN. Finn. My name is Finn.

VICTORIA. Finn, as in?

FINN. Finn as in finished. Hello. Welcome to the abattoir.

VICTORIA. Is that how you say it?

MISSY. Didn't I come through?

FINN. A doll. Max? Can I speak to you, Max? In my room.

MAX. Ladies, we'll be just a second. Please, what's ours is yours.

(MAX *and* FINN *exit into* FINN*'s room. Smiling,* FINN *shuts the door. The women take in the room.*)

FINN. Who are these women?

MAX. The craps table. I told you.

VICTORIA. When you called I didn't know if you were serious. I'm staying with Sandra and Dave...I looked at the clock...I thought it might be...I dunno.

MISSY. I remember what you said...I know you need the money. You're lucky. I was looking out for you.

FINN. You lied to me. I can't believe...wait, yes I can!

VICTORIA. You have no idea...Where did you find these two?

MISSY. I was just about to get off and then Max gave me a hundred dollar tip...I thought...end of the month. My aunt was able to watch Katie.

MAX. Missy is a piece of work, isn't she? And the other one is like a cool breeze on a hot subway platform.

FINN. Those women...It's like a Jay McInerney novel exploded in there.

(MISSY *and* VICTORIA *primp themselves.* MISSY *hands* VICTORIA *a stack of bills or envelope.*)

MISSY. For you.

    (**VICTORIA** *looks at the money.*)

    What? Take it. That's just part, the rest after…

    (**VICTORIA** *reluctantly takes the money.*)

FINN. No fucking way. I'm not doing this.

MAX. Just have a good time. It's your bachelor party. Think of her as a hidden track…

MISSY. Oh, baby, don't be nervous. Just be your charming self. Have a drink.

VICTORIA. Is that what you do?

FINN. No. No.

MAX. Then…If you're going to be an asshole, just give me back the chips.

FINN. Fine.

VICTORIA. I'm…nevermind.

MAX. What are you going to tell Susan?

FINN. I lost it.

MAX. You're going to tell her you lost ten grand?

FINN. Just shut up. I need to think.

    (**MISSY** *stares at* **VICTORIA.**)

MISSY. You told me you'd done this before? Look, sister, the first time…the first time is… *(unsaid "hard")*.

VICTORIA. Yeah.

FINN. Nothing is going to happen with me and that…her.

MAX. I don't care…but you're going have enjoy yourself.

    (**FINN** *stares at the chips.*)

MISSY. We hand it out for free most of the time…All it takes is a hot shower and a new morning and you'll never think twice.

VICTORIA. You're a good friend, Missy.

MISSY. These two are soft…still keep an eye on each other, and remember to smile.

    (**FINN** *breaking from the trance.*)

FINN. Will it end tonight?

MAX. After tonight.

(**MAX** *returns to his room.* **FINN** *lingers, places the chips back in his pocket – before entering the party. The party takes on a life of its own. The dialogue should have a quick pace, almost on top of each other.*)

MISSY. Come in and relax Max. Relax Max...get it? Ha ha.

MAX. It's like Christmas came early, look at you girls. See, Finn? We doubled down...

FINN. They are a sight. Max, you're good at few things – very, very few things – but at starting a party, you're fucking Mozart.

MAX. That's the spirit. You're in good hands. Now, ladies, what can we do to you?

FINN. *For* you, he means...

MAX. No I don't.

(**FINN** *makes his best attempt to turn back time, to be his old partying self. The group all continue to do drugs and drink – touch and flirt – until they don't.*)

FINN. How are you Victoria? Victoria! That's my favorite Kinks' song. Are you a fan of...? Never mind.

(*She smiles, not knowing.*)

VICTORIA. *(to* **FINN***)* Nice room you've got here, Max.

FINN. I'm Finn.

VICTORIA. Nicer than the Tropicana.

MISSY. This how the other half lives?

MAX. The top two percent, please. Only the best for my friends...

FINN. Can I get you girls something to drink? You name it?

VICTORIA. Vodka?

FINN. Do we have vodka? I think we have it all. Max?

MISSY. Who's got the blow?!

MAX. I like the way you think, Missy. A one track mind... Let's skip the appetizers and get straight to the main course.

FINN. This all seems familiar...

MAX. ...Deja vu....

FINN. ...So, do you girls normally roam the halls of this fine establishment knocking on doors and depending on the kindness of strangers?

VICTORIA. Not always. Never...

FINN. ...Lucky us...

VICTORIA. So, is this a convention or something?

MAX. This? We do this every year. It's a reunion.

MISSY. Like school?

MAX. A family reunion. Would you believe that the two of us are brothers?

MISSY. You didn't tell me that!

VICTORIA. Oh. *(trying)* I see that.

FINN. Really? You need to get your eyes checked. We're nothing alike...

MAX. ...That's what he keeps telling himself. But, you can't choose your family, can you, Missy?

MISSY. I don't know. I think you can choose anything you want.

FINN. That's right, Missy.

(FINN *does a line.*)

Yes! Here we go...

MAX. Look who's back. I can see it now.

FINN. ...Just trying to get that feeling I remember. That running through clouds feeling. Can't find it.

MISSY. Don't worry. We'll find it, right Vic?

(VIC *says nothing, perhaps a forced smile.*)

We'll find it.

VICTORIA. So, what do you boys do?

MAX. I do drugs. I sell them. I do them.

MISSY. Ha ha. Drugs. Get it? You're funny...

VICTORIA. What about you?

MAX. Finn is a podiatrist...

FINN. ...No...

MAX. ...actually, Finn is a writer, he writes graphic novels.

VICTORIA. Really? I love graphic novels.

FINN. Fuck. There...No. I'm not a writer either.

MAX. Oh yeah, you quit. Gee, Finn what are you?

FINN. I'm just trying to be...The truth is I'm a teacher. That's not the truth...not yet...I work at the Columbia University library...I make ten dollars an hour.

VICTORIA. Teacher, huh? I remember I wanted to be a teacher when I was little. When I was a little girl I thought all my teachers where so pretty...so womanly...just seemed right...

MISSY. Yeah, I remember that too...

MAX. Well, I wanted to be fucking G.I. Joe and Don Mattingly, but that didn't happen.

MISSY. You can be whatever you want tonight, baby.

MAX. Oh yeah? I think we got the picks of the litter here...

FINN. ...They're not animals, Max...

MAX. ...I didn't say they were...

FINN. You implied it.

MAX. Of course not. It's a saying. I'm sorry, did I offend you girls?

MISSY. I don't think so. Did you?

VICTORIA. Not me.

MAX. Finn here is a little jumpy around new people. Everybody is having a good time, right?

FINN. I'm sorry. I haven't partied in a long time.

MAX. Finn has been sick. But he is feeling much better now.

VICTORIA. What sorta sick?

FINN. Nothing to worry about. Max is trying to be funny. Enough about me. Please. So, Victoria, how do you know Missy here?

MISSY. Vic used to work at the Trop with me...

FINN. No longer, huh..?

VICTORIA. It wasn't just me…That place. Six weeks ago. Place is empty when people have money, and right now people don't have money – not for AC it's not Vegas – fewer visitors – less tips. They laid off a bunch of girls. Missy has been there longer so they kept her…

MISSY. Don't remind me. Five years in August.

MAX. We're not here to talk about work. Come on, we're bringing down the whole room.

FINN. .What do you want to talk about?

MAX. Who said I wanted to talk?

(MAX *pulls* MISSY *to his lap.*)

Hello.

MISSY. *(giggling)* Hi.

(MAX *and* MISSY *engage.*)

FINN. Money is important, isn't it? Just so unbelievably necessary. Like air – like if you don't have it you just might suffocate. I'm really sorry to hear about the job. It's tough all over…The recession is…

(MAX *breaks from his necking.*)

MAX. Did you just say "the recession?!" Ugh…anybody empty?

MISSY. My turn.

(MISSY *gets up to get a drink.*)

It's okay, we keep care of each other.

VICTORIA. Mother superior.

MISSY. I took her under my wing…how long?

VICTORIA. From the beginning. I just moved to the city last year.

FINN. The city?

VICTORIA. Atlantic City.

(FINN *laughs.*)

FINN. You think this is a city?

VICTORIA. From where I came from…from Lenoir, North Carolina, it's a city. We were headed to New York but…

FINN. We?

VICTORIA. Jack and me...

MISSY. I don't think these guys want to hear about your ex, Vic...

MAX. No one cares. All that's important is that you're here now...

VICTORIA. ...Sorry. I do that...

FINN. ...It's okay. I care...I care...Jack?

VICTORIA. He left as soon as we got here. Some people can't handle the lights. I said I'm not...no way, never.

FINN. Well, that's shitty...

MAX. ...Depends. I guess...

MISSY. ...Good riddance, I say...

FINN. ...It doesn't depend on anything. He was a stupid... It's shitty. Real men don't walk away...they don't...

MAX. Jesus Christ. Look, Dr. Sweater Vest, your idea of manhood doesn't exist... Sorry, girls...Finn is selling you a Unicorn.

FINN. Max has a philosophy or mantra or...don't worry, he'll tell you all about it...

MAX. *(getting warmed up)* There's one type of man. A best man. Right, Finn? *(beat)* A best man?

FINN. Just stop. I have an idea! Let's have some entertainment. Max, give the ladies your best Mick Jagger.

MAX. Finn. We have company.

FINN. You know the rules. Anywhere. Anytime.

MAX. No. Not tonight.

FINN. But...But, there are rules...aren't there? We have to play by the rules, isn't that right, Max? Otherwise... what? Chaos. That reminds me...How many points are Missy and Victoria here?

VICTORIA. Points?

MAX. New rules. New game.

VICTORIA. Oohh, a game! What game?

MAX. It's called...it's called, "Remember When?"

VICTORIA. I don't know that one...

MAX. It's just like "This is Your Life."

MISSY. How do you play?

MAX. You just...don't forget. I'll go first. "Remember when..." I was having a good time, just now with you, Missy? Come here.

(**MAX,** *not wanting to let the party falter, playfully gropes* **MISSY.**)

MISSY. Don't worry, I remember...

(**FINN** *goes to the drugs.*)

FINN. How could we forget? How can anyone forget? Might need a lobotomy, right, Vic? Just cut it all out...

(**FINN** *does some coke and downs his drink.*)

Just burn it all away...

(**MAX** *notices the excess.*)

MAX. Relax, Len Bias.

FINN. I know what I'm doing. Not my first rodeo. Remember when...my turn...

MAX. ...I thought you didn't want to play...

FINN. ...now I do. I want to play. "Remember when" I had to write all those papers for you, Max, just to get you through Writing workshop? Just think, without my help...no job, no fancy room...none of this money he throws around...

MAX. Oh. I remember when, this one time, I had a good night at the tables...made all this money and, being a generous sort, gave it away...to this charity.

MISSY. How nice.

MAX. Yep, a charity that helps people who are down on their luck and have nowhere else to turn. You know, losers.

FINN. Oh, you are magnanimous.

(**MAX** *shoots him a confused look.*)

VICTORIA. Oh, it's not a bad thing.

(FINN laughs.)

MAX. Whatever. I'm not going to apologize for winning.

FINN. Oh yeah, I forgot, it's all luck...just dumb, DUMB luck. It has to be...because it certainly isn't talent.

(silence)

MAX. Anybody hungry? I know a great little place called "The Munch Box."

FINN. *(checking his watch)* It's closed. Remember when? Remember when, I dumped Amber Thomas freshman year...

MAX. ...Boring...

FINN. ...You called her Larry Bird...

MAX. ...She was really tall...

FINN. ...She was a girl. That fucked her up, man. I liked her. I broke her fucking heart. But *I* didn't do it. You did.

VICTORIA. That's terrible.

FINN. Well, ladies, if you want to know how a man is going to treat you, look at how he treats his mother...am I right?

(MAX stares at FINN.)

MAX. Okay. Let's keep playing...

FINN. *(realizing)* No. I'm sorry. That's enough...

(MAX does another blast of coke.)

MAX. Come on, we're just starting. Remember when...? Finn, here's a story...something only I know...you wanna play this fucking game with me? *(stopping himself)* Nevermind. Anyway, for my job, my...I travel...lots of driving. Leased cars. Miles and miles. On these trips I'll listen to the radio a lot...And this is the truth, the other day...The other day, more than just the other day – many days, recently, I found myself listening to a classics station. You know the station where you find the Doobie Brothers playing on loop. Why am I listening to an oldies station? Not because I wanted to hear

Mungo fucking Jerry....no, because they were playing fucking PEARL JAM. Pearl Jam and Nirvana and
fucking Pavement. The Pixies don't get old. *(beat)* Is it
me? Because if that's old, then that means I'm old...
and I'm not old. Fuck I'm not even...Fuck it. The sun
sets in the east, cats love water, Germans are cuddly...
Everything I know to be false is actually true. But, this
is not true. Not this...So I ask you...In the name of all
things holy, do the Pixies get old?

VICTORIA. Who are the Pixies?

MAX. Fuck.

FINN. Everything gets old, Max.

MAX. Yeah. You know, I work for a big drug company,
make all this money, right? She asked me...when she
was really sick...She asked me if I knew of any experi-
mental drug that could help her. Help me, she says.
I couldn't. A cancer cure? *(laughing to himself, drowning in emotions)* You got acne? No problem – fixed.
Thinning hair? Done. Fucking heartburn? I can help
you, Mom. Cancer? Sorry, Mom. I'm sorry. It was too
late. Fuck. I'm sorry to get all faggy on you guys.

MISSY. You alright?

MAX. Good as gold.

FINN. In vino veritas.

MAX. Yeah, whatever. We're out of ice.

(**MAX** *grabs the ice bucket and goes to the door.*)

I'll only be a minute. Talk amongst yourselves.

(**MAX** *exits.*)

(*With* **MAX** *gone, the energy falls, an awkward silence.*)

FINN. Nature calls.

(**FINN** *gets up to go to the bathroom.*)

MISSY. *(to* **VICTORIA***)* What?

VICTORIA. Jesus, this is...I don't know, Missy.

MISSY. Divide and conquer, sister. Let's get this done. I have
to be home in the morning, Lynn is gonna kill me and

I have to work again tomorrow night because Marcy switched with me...

VICTORIA. These guys...Is it always this way?

MISSY. Try not just sitting there. Warm him up a little.

VICTORIA. Then?

(MISSY *laughs.*)

MISSY. No checks, no plastic. These guys are a gold mine, and they seem nice enough. Besides, the rate these guys are going...they're going to pass out before...try to get him to lay down...

VICTORIA. ...I know when you called...

MISSY. ...Don't even think about leaving me here alone. Vicky, you don't know this yet...but you don't find a lot of grace in survival.

(VICTORIA *looks at* MISSY.)

VICTORIA. Okay. I feel flush.

MISSY. I don't have time to baby-sit you. Just do what you have to do. We leave together.

(FINN *returns from the bathroom.*)

FINN. As much fun as this is, I might need to...

(MAX *returns with ice.*)

MAX. I'm a new man. Did you miss me?

MISSY. You know it. What's next on the agenda, boys?

FINN. I just need to sit.

(*A shaky* FINN *sits on the bed.*)

MISSY. Max, you wanna be alone with me?

MAX. Whatever Finn wants. Finn?

FINN. Don't let me hold you back.

(MISSY *stares at* VICTORIA.)

I'm pretty fucked up. I think. I dunno.

MISSY. Will you dance with me, Max?

MAX. No music.

MISSY. Sure there is…

(*She embraces him.* MISSY *takes* MAX *and they slow dance real close and awkwardly. An eighth grade shuffle of a dance.*)

(MISSY, *taking the lead, kisses* MAX.)

(VICTORIA *joins* FINN *on the bed, they look at each other.*)

VICTORIA. Do you want to kiss me?

FINN. Yes. I'm married.

VICTORIA. You're married?

FINN. Guilty as charged.

VICTORIA. No need to feel guilty. It's Atlantic City…I really don't care.

(VICTORIA *and* FINN *share a light, almost sweet, kiss.*)

MAX. How do you feel?

FINN. I got it…I'm running in clouds. (*to* VICTORIA) I feel so…old and so young all at once. You're really pretty.

(MAX *and* MISSY *become more heated.*)

VICTORIA. Let's see your room, give them some privacy.

FINN. I guess we should.

MAX. You don't have to go.

FINN. It's that time.

MISSY. You be good to my girl. Everybody play nice.

(FINN *turns and goes with* VICTORIA *to the adjoining door, lingering at the entrance.*)

MAX. You're welcome.

(FINN *shuts the adjoining door.* MISSY *and* MAX *start to kiss. It becomes heated.*)

(*In* FINN*'s room,* FINN *and* VICTORIA *kiss each other, it only goes so far…then is halted.*)

FINN. Jesus, you're shaking.

VICTORIA. So do you wanna…what do you wanna do?

FINN. I don't…

VICTORIA. Your friend paid.

FINN. I don't want to do anything.

VICTORIA. Really?

FINN. Really.

VICTORIA. That's...Can I just sit for a second?

(In MAX*'s room,* MAX *and* MISSY *break from a heated embrace.)*

MISSY. You're a good kisser. So you know. I'm not a whore, or nothing. Neither is... *(unsaid "Victoria")* We're just poor. It's...it's just so hard, you understand? But this is fun. I'm going to make myself look special for you.

*(*MISSY *saunters into the bathroom.)*

VICTORIA. You're a nice guy. What are you doing here?

FINN. I don't know.

VICTORIA. I know...sometimes you just look up and there you are. This isn't me.

FINN. I know.

*(*VICTORIA *weeps briefly...regaining composure.)*

VICTORIA. Can I use your...

*(*FINN *nods "yes."* VICTORIA *goes to the door, stopping...)*

I gotta wait here for Missy. *(beat)* The things we do for money, huh?

*(*VICTORIA *exits into* FINN*'s bathroom.)*

*(*FINN, *stunned by the final words, charges into* MAX*'s room.* MAX *sits up.)*

FINN. I need to talk to you.

MAX. Jesus Christ, Missy is in the bathroom. What are you doing?

FINN. I need to talk to you.

*(*FINN *takes the chips and drops them on the bed.)*

MAX. You're fucking wasted. Regulate.

FINN. She's a person.

MAX. That's good, Finn. Yes, she is...

FINN. I'm done. *This* is done. I don't want your money and I don't want...this anymore. If I can't afford school, then I won't go...and you know what? It doesn't matter – because I'll have my soul and I'll have Susan.

MAX. Take the fucking diapers off, Finn...

FINN. You're this knife, Max, you cut until you hit bone. But, not again, not to Susan.

MAX. You wanna blame me for all your fucking problems? Great. But, you know what kills you? You. You kills you...

FINN. ...Our friendship was the most important thing in the world to me...Fuck everybody else. They didn't exist...but now every glimpse I recall of us makes me sick...

MAX. You. I came here needing you. For the first time, I needed you, not the other way around...and I still end up giving you everything – everything you're screaming for, even if you don't know it. The truth. Yeah, maybe I'm stupid...you've always made it so clear how stupid you think I am...but I haven't squirreled myself away from the world because I'm scared of it. Have some guts.

FINN. I don't have guts. You're right about that...I never have. Why do you think I quit writing? My writing sucked because I couldn't look myself in the eye and say, "This is who I am." Well, this is who I am *now*...and I could do it without you...but you can't do *any of this* without me. It's tomorrow...that's what scares you, isn't it? Tomorrow. All by yourself. But you can't escape it... It'll come. Tomorrow I'm going to wake up with my wife.

MAX. Finn, it's me.

FINN. I know. We never really shared anything other than living next to one another in a dorm. Names pulled from a hat...Goodbye.

(Silence. **MAX** *is speechless for perhaps the first time.* **FINN** *goes to the adjoining door.* **MAX** *stirs from his stunned condition.)*

MAX. I haven't always been honest with you. In fact, I was dishonest with you tonight.

FINN. What?

MAX. *(calm)* I *did* fuck Susan. I fucked her in the bathroom of the club the first night we met her...and almost every night for weeks after that. I didn't tell you at the time, because I knew you had a thing for her. She was...filthy.

FINN. Oh.

MAX. That was the only time I ever lied to you. Now you know, and I want you to remember it every time you look her in the eyes...I want you to think about it deeply, and know it's the truth. She told me not to tell you earlier on the phone. She called it our little secret.

FINN. Oh.

MAX. That's all you have to say? Oh?

(silence)

FINN. I knew. Like you said, I'm not stupid.

MAX. That's it?

FINN. Do you expect me to be surprised?

MAX. Fight back.

*(***MAX** *approaches* **FINN** *pushing and taunting him.)*

Punch my fucking face in. Punch me in the face... It'd be the first honest thing...You bitch. You woman. You...DO SOMETHING! YOU FUCKING JOKE! DO SOMETHING, FINN!

*(***FINN** *pushes* **MAX** *back.)*

FINN. Now I know for certain...and I don't care. Do you hear me?

*(***FINN** *turns his back to* **MAX,** *about to leave.)*

*(***MAX** *lights a cigarette.)*

MAX. We got in trouble too.

FINN. What do you mean?

MAX. She got pregnant.

FINN. I'm sorry?

MAX. Susan. Back then. We got rid of it.

FINN. No.

MAX. It was just something that happened.

FINN. No. That's…

> (*A stunned* FINN, *unable to articulate anymore, slowly picks up the chips from where they've fallen.*)

MAX. What are you doing?

FINN. I earned these.

> (FINN *exits into his room.*)

MAX. Finn…?

> (FINN *stands in his room, stunned. He is a broken man.*)

> (*In* MAX's *room,* MAX *destroys the room. He knocks* MISSY's *purse to the ground. Picking up its contents, placing them back in the purse, he stares at a photo that has fallen out. Then, he weeps over it.*)

> (*A second passes and* MISSY *returns from the bathroom, she is hardly dressed.*)

> (*In* FINN's *room,* VICTORIA *returns.*)

> (*The first beams of a new morning can be seen peering through the windows.*)

MISSY. Is everything alright?

VICTORIA. Is Missy still here?

MISSY. I heard shouting so I took my time.

MAX. Is this your daughter?

MISSY. Yes.

VICTORIA. Look, you're fucked up, why don't you lay down, shut your eyes and relax.

MAX. Is she…sick?

MISSY. Yes.

MAX. You're a good mom? Right?

(**MISSY** *goes to* **MAX**. **VICTORIA** *goes to* **FINN**.)

VICTORIA. Just relax.

(**FINN** *says nothing.* **MISSY** *goes to the windows, which are now flooded with the day's first light. She starts to pull the curtains, but lingers before pulling them tight.*)

MISSY. Dawn even makes Atlantic City beautiful. Like a whole new world.

(**MISSY** *takes one last glance, then shuts the blinds.*)

MAX. I just need a little while. I'm so tired. I can't stop thinking…

(**MAX** *drops his head in his hands.*)

(**VICTORIA** *moves a distraught* **FINN** *to the bed, trying to get him to lay down.*)

VICTORIA. You Relax…Relax, Max. Just relax Max.

FINN. *(stunned)* I…I'm not *(unspoken "him")*.

(**FINN** *slowly approaches* **VICTORIA** *and kisses her – dead-lipped. It escalates quickly.*)

(**FINN** *takes* **VICTORIA** *by the throat and, turning her over, he instigates rough sex – bordering on rape – with her. The sex is mechanical and violent – a release.*)

(**FINN** *comes. Emotionally exhausted – scared by what has happened –* **FINN** *moves to the edge of the bed.*)

You should go.

(**MAX** *lays in the fetal position, his head in* **MISSY**'s *lap. She strokes his hair.*)

MAX. I need a little while…

MISSY. It's okay. It's your dime. It's okay, baby.

(**VICTORIA,** *shaken by the incident – gathers her things and slowly goes toward the door.*)

FINN. Take these.

(*FINN* hands **VICTORIA** *the chips.*)

VICTORIA. I…

FINN. Take them and go. Don't look back.

(**VICTORIA** *takes the chips and exits.*)

(**MISSY** *closes her eyes and continues to stroke* **MAX***'s hair.*)

MISSY. What do you want me to say?

MAX. Anything.

(**FINN** *picks up his phone and dials.*)

MISSY. What am I supposed to do?

(**FINN** *does not speak into the phone.*)

I'm sorry…I can't think of anything…

(*Lights fade to black out.*)

(*Pixies' "Wave of Mutilation [UK Surf]" plays.**)

End of Play

---

*Please see Music Use Note page 3.

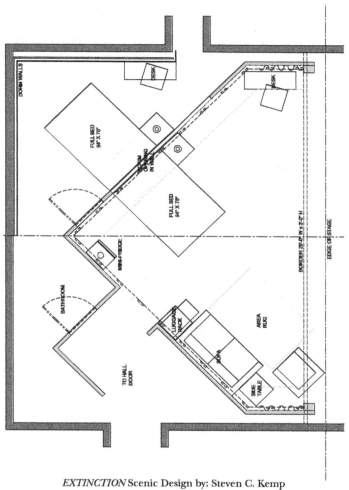

EXTINCTION Scenic Design by: Steven C. Kemp

OTHER TITLES AVAILABLE FROM SAMUEL FRENCH

OFF OFF BRADWAY FESTIVAL PLAYS, 33RD SERIES

Various Authors

One of Manhattan's most established play festivals, the Samuel French Off-Off Broadway Short Play Festival fosters the work of young writers, giving them the exposure of publication and representation.

The festival resulting in this collection was held July 15th-20th, 2008 at the Peter Jay Sharp Theatre on 42nd Street in New York City.

From the initial submission pool, approximately 50 plays were chosen to be performed over a period of one week. A panel of judges comprised of New York area theater professionals, critics, and educators nominated one or more of each evening's plays as finalists. The final round was then held on the last day of the Festival. Out of these plays, six winners listed below were chosen by Samuel French, Inc. to receive publication and licensing contracts.

Winning plays in this collection include:
F*cking Art by Bekah Brunstetter
Ayravana Flies or A Pretty Dish by Sheila Callaghan
The Thread Men by Thomas C. Dunn
The Dying Breed by Thomas Higgins
The Grave by Gabe McKinley
Juniper; Jubilee by Janine Nabers

OTHER TITLES AVAILABLE FROM SAMUEL FRENCH

KINDNESS

Adam Rapp

Drama / 2m, 2f / Interior

An ailing mother and her teenaged son flee Illinois and a crumbling marriage for the relative calm and safety of a midtown Manhattan hotel. Mom holds tickets to a popular musical about love among bohemians. Her son isn't interested, so Mom takes the kindly cabdriver instead, while the boy entertains a visitor from down the hall, an enigmatic, potentially dangerous young woman.

Kindness is a play about the possibility for sympathy in a harsh world and the meaning of mercy in the face of devastating circumstances.

Premiered at Playwrights Horizons, New York City in 2008.

"Compelling. A well-crafted mini-thriller, which keeps you in suspense until the final blackout."
– Joe Dziemianowics, *New York Daily News*

"Rapp has raised some provocative questions about the prickly mother/son relationship he has drawn in such detail."
– Marilyn Stasio, *Variety*

"Pungent, vivid...Rapp finds a gentle approach to his characters' physical and emotional pain without turning sentimental. His playful side is on display too." [Four Stars]
– Diane Snyder, *Time Out New York*

"Adam Rapp can write dense, tense, funny dialogue."
– Charles Isherwood, *The New York Times*

"A taut and involving dark comedy. Hilarious and unsettling."
– Dan Bacalzo, *TheatreMania.com*

OTHER TITLES AVAILABLE FROM SAMUEL FRENCH

STAIN

Tony Glazer

Drama / 4m, 3f / Unit Set

Comedy / 3m, 3f

Stain follows 15-year-old Thomas through his quickly-crumbling life and the secrets his family tries to keep at bay. In this darkly comic piece about the complexities of family, Thomas is confronted with a choice that will either save or mark him forever.

"Hilariously revolting...snappily written...Glazer's play's will continue to be worth watching."
– *Variety*

DUST

Billy Goda

Thriller / 4m, 1f, with doubling

Dust is an edge-of-your-seat thriller. Martin is an executive with money and a paunch. Zeke, a gifted young man torn down by drugs, is an ex-con with street smarts and a minimum wage position. Early one morning, in the fitness center of the Essex House, a battle-of-wills begins over the most trivial of requests. As described in *The New York Times* review: "Verbal sparring turns angry, posturing leads to entrenched positions, and out of nothing - out of dust - a grudge match is born." Once Martin's daughter Jenny becomes entangled, the stakes are raised even higher - escalating a war for respect into one for revenge and ultimately survival. Who will be standing when the dust settles?

"Great theatre! It's fun, it's exciting, it's electric, it makes you understand why theater is so special."
–WOR Radio

"THRILLS in *DUST!* EXCELLENT ACTING AND WRITING laced with mordant humor."
– *Associated Press*

"*Dust* begins with a struggle over power and respect. Verbal sparring turns angry, posturing leads to entrenched positions, and out of nothing – out of dust – a grudge match is born. Billy Goda tells his story in short, sharp scenes, each with a clear dramatic idea."
– *The New York Times*

"NYC THEATRE PICK"
– *Newsday*